Dear Parent:

Your child's love of reading starts here!

Every child learns to read in a different way and at his or her own speed. Some go back and forth between reading levels and read favorite books again and again. Others read through each level in order. You can help your young reader improve and become more confident by encouraging his or her own interests and abilities. From books your child reads with you to the first books he or she reads alone, there are I Can Read Books for every stage of reading:

SHARED READING

Basic language, word repetition, and whimsical illustrations, ideal for sharing with your emergent reader

BEGINNING READING

Short sentences, familiar words, and simple concepts for children eager to read on their own

READING WITH HELP

Engaging stories, longer sentences, and language play for developing readers

READING ALONE

Complex plots, challenging vocabulary, and high-interest topics for the independent reader

I Can Read Books have introduced children to the joy of reading since 1957. Featuring award-winning authors and illustrators and a fabulous cast of beloved characters, I Can Read Books set the standard for beginning readers.

A lifetime of discovery begins with the magical words "I Can Read!"

Visit www.icanread.com for information
on enriching your child's reading experience.

Magic Mixies: A Mixed-Up Adventure
Copyright © 2023 The Moose Group. MAGIC MIXIES MIXLINGS™ logos, names
and characters are licensed trade marks of Moose Enterprises (INT) Pty Ltd.
All rights reserved. Printed in the United States of America.
No part of this book may be used or reproduced in any manner whatsoever without written permission
except in the case of brief quotations embodied in critical articles and reviews.
For information address HarperCollins Children's Books, a division of HarperCollins Publishers,
195 Broadway, New York, NY 10007.
www.icanread.com

Library of Congress Control Number: 2023930375
ISBN 978-0-06-331090-2
Book design by Stephanie Hays

23 24 25 26 27   LB   10 9 8 7 6 5 4 3 2 1
First Edition

Magic MIXIES™ MIXLINGS™

A Mixed-Up Adventure

Adapted by Mickey Domenici
Based on the Episodes
"Feeling Enchanted," "Camp Critter Talent Show,"
and "Escape Cave" written by Katie Chilson

HARPER
An Imprint of HarperCollinsPublishers

Mixia is a secret world

full of creatures,

like Magic Mixies

and Mixlings.

They each have amazing powers.

Sienna is lost in Mixia.

Luckily, Carrot and the Mixlings
are helping her find the Castle
so she can go home.

But it hasn't been smooth sailing.

First, the friends must pass through
a town named Enchanters Edge.
Sienna uses the wand to sail
the raft there.

Carrot says it's a beautiful place
full of happy Mixlings.
But when they arrive,
everyone is grumpy!

7

It won't stop raining.

The bridge on the way to

the Castle is underwater.

Sienna casts a spell

to stop the storm, but it fails.

Oh no, they are stuck!

Carrot says the magic storm is controlled by the grumpy Mixlings.

If the friends can cheer everyone up,

the storm will stop.

Sienna is ready for the challenge!

Geckler can light a cozy fire.

Luggle makes yummy cocoa.

Pixly loves the sound

of raindrops while napping.

The Mixlings realize you
can have lots of fun when it rains.
They put on some music
and dance indoors.

The friends are having so much fun,
it stops the magic storm!
The sunshine is warm and bright.
They cross the bridge and
continue to the Castle.

After they leave Enchanters Edge,
the friends come to a snowy tundra.
It's so cold that they are all shivering.
They decide to pitch a tent and light
a fire.

This reminds the Mixlings
of Camp Critter.

Geckler explains that Camp Critter
is a summer camp just for Mixlings.

His favorite part was the talent show!

Sienna thinks that sounds like fun.

She uses the wand to make a stage.

Pixly juggles snowballs . . .

but they melt!

Luggle stretches to catch popcorn . . .

but there is too much to catch!

Dawne does a ribbon dance . . .

but wind blows everyone away!

Something is wrong.

Sienna casts a spell to find out

what is causing the chaos.

It is Parlo!

But why, Parlo?

Parlo says she feels bad

because she doesn't have a talent.

Sienna understands how Parlo feels.

When she came to Mixia,

Sienna thought she didn't belong either.

But she was brave and learned magic.

Parlo can be brave too.

With Sienna's help,

Parlo is ready to perform.

Parlo gets on stage.

She asks everyone to hold paws.

Parlo turns them invisible.

Everyone loves Parlo's talent.

Parlo apologizes for ruining

their acts with magic.

Pixly gives Parlo a big hug.

The next morning,

the friends set off for the Castle.

They find themselves in a dark forest.

It's full of dangerous electricity.

Worse, Luggle's tummy feels sick.

The friends need to find somewhere safe

for Luggle to rest.

They start to run!

Geckler finds a cave just in time.

Phew!

But the cave is actually an escape room.

The friends have to solve puzzles.

There's one more door to unlock

when Luggle gets sick all over it!

But magic comes out,

and it opens the door.

On the other side of the door
is the Castle!
They finally made it.

This mixed-up adventure
is complete . . . for now!

Magicus Mixus!

Magic ingredients are hidden in the pages.

Can you find them all?